VINDICTIVE JUSTICE

I AM MY BROTHER'S KEEPER

DANTE PEREZ

Cover design by: Ira-Rebeca
Printed in the United States of America

CONTENTS

CHAPTER ONE

A Thorn in the American Dream

The clouds were beginning to roll in and the wind had picked up, kicking up sand along the shoreline and onto everyone at the beach. People were busy scurrying to pick up their tents and other belongings before the storm moved into Paloma.

"Eric!"

I turned around and shot my hands up just in the nick of time to catch the football spiraling directly towards my head.

"Hey, knucklehead! Do you know just how close you were to getting your ass kicked right now? That was an inch away from my face."

"Yeah, yeah, man. Had to wake you up 'cause you're over there daydreaming when we're supposed to be making the most of this day. You know I hardly get any time off now. And on another note, just because you're older than me doesn't mean you can kick my ass. Don't forget those whoopins I would give you when we were younger and Mom had to pull us apart."

"OK, Mr. Hotshot. You think because you did a few years in the big house you can easily bully me around now?" I threw the ball back at Mark and ran towards him at full speed, and just as I figured, he backed down instantly.

"All right, all right! Chill! I'm not tryin' to ruin my new shirt."

"New shirt?" I poked my finger through one of the holes.

Mark turned and pushed my hand away. "It was on sale. Come on, let's sit down and eat somethin' before it starts to rain. Archer! Kate! Get over here!" My niece and nephew came racing from the swings as fast as their little legs could carry them.

"Kate, you want mayo on your sandwich? Archer, tell your uncle Eric to fix yours up for you."

"All right, Archie. Extra pickles, right?" He nodded. "Remember I'm still waiting on that list of things you want for your birthday. Just go easy on me, fella. And tell your dad to help you write it and not do it for you since I know you need to practice your writing. It's better if you're ahead of the other kids when school starts again. Honestly, I probably won't be able to tell the difference between your handwriting and his."

"Kate, sit at the other table next to us, and take your brother. I need to talk to your uncle for a second."

"What's up, man? Everything OK?" Mark wasn't the type of guy to sit you down and have a serious talk, so I couldn't help but be a little concerned. I knew he was finally back on the right path after so many years of fighting his demons, but nonetheless there's nothing I still wouldn't have done for him even then to make sure he and his kids didn't lose sight of that happiness.

"I ran into—" He turned around to make sure Archie and Kate weren't listening. "I ran into Vicky yesterday at the grocery store and—"

"Vicky! What the hell is she doing back in town?"

"Hey man, not so loud. Look, I know you hate her after everything that's happened, but she's still the kids' mom."

"And you think she deserves a little bit of respect still?" I couldn't help but shake my head and look away. *Hate* was an understatement. There are plenty of things you can use the word *hate* for, like hating when you step in dog crap, hating pineapple on pizza, or hating when your team loses the World Series, but what I felt for her was so much stronger than hate.

"She somehow found out about my new job at the refinery and started talkin' about how much she's been missing me, saying she wishes we could get back together and give it another shot."

"I'll give her a real nice shot for you if you want, right between the eyes." He let out a chuckle, giving me some hope that he wasn't even going to entertain the thought of them having another chance in hell. "I bet she was tweaked out too, huh?"

"Eric"—he looked me directly in the eyes—"I don't want you to worry about it. Seriously. I'm happy the way things are going right now and I'm not gonna let anything ruin it for me, and especially not for the kids. I'm not going to let her anywhere near 'em."

"Well, I'm glad to hear that, I really am. But I know how close you guys were and—"

"*Were*. You said it yourself. Everything's changed. I've changed." There was a seriousness in his tone I had rarely heard.

"I just wish we never had to speak about her again, much less run into her. Hell, I can't even believe she's still alive. How long has it been since we last saw her?"

"I know; I felt like I had to get it off my chest and tell someone about it. It's a little hard sometimes, you know? I really want a mother there for the kids ... so we can go to the park, to the movies, to go get ice cream. Instead, well, look at me, I'm out here hanging out with you."

"Very sweet of you, man. Very sweet. Well, you know you can always count on me, Bro. I tell you one thing though, if I ever run into her, she better not come up to me with any of that nonsense. She's not fooling *me*. And I do trust you. I trust that you'd do anything to protect those kids. And I might not say this a lot, but I'm really proud of you. I know you've come a long way and conquered all of your obstacles. This new job is a blessing. She knows that, and she wants to use it to support her habit."

"I know. It's not gonna happen, I promise you that. I really wanted to give you a heads-up so it didn't catch you off guard. Knowing you, you'd run into her and pop her in the face thinking you saw a ghost ... or for the hell of it. But hey, I'm actually kinda seein' someone already, but we can talk about that another time." He got up to throw his trash away. "Come on, kids. You guys ready to go? Finish up."

"Whoa, slow down, man. Give them some time to chew their food. So who's the unlucky lady?" I asked. "Or guy, knowing you."

"*She* is someone you'll probably meet pretty soon. I'll hit you up next weekend and we can all get together and maybe take the kids out on the lake. Maybe I'll bring her along. Actually, the kids haven't even met her yet either. You down for some fishing?"

"Does *V* smoke crack? Of course." I could never help myself when it came to cracking jokes; it was my passion and field of expertise. Seeing Mark laugh was a good sign. I knew he was moving on and couldn't have been happier for him.

◆ ◆ ◆

On the drive home, the thought of Vicky being back in town was stuck in my mind. This wasn't someone I just had a random grudge against because she had said something I didn't agree with, looked at me the wrong way, or 'cause we had our political differences; it went far beyond that.

She and Mark met their junior year in school and became high school sweethearts. They were inseparable like a real-life Romeo and Juliet, if you will. Soon after they graduated they ended up getting married in the town's old chapel and about a year after that little Kate was born. Our mother couldn't have been more thrilled. It was her first grandchild, her pride and joy. Mark picked up a job at Dad's machine shop to help them buy diapers and take care of his responsibilities. By the time you knew it they were closing a deal on their first house. They had everything going for them: a precious little girl, a stable and well-paying job, and a beautiful new home, the American Dream. But every dream must come to an end aside from our everlasting one. And after a fairy tale dream like that there's only one way you seem to go and that's downhill.

Vicky had begun hanging out with Brenda frequently, one of her old friends from school who had always been nothing but a bad influence, and Mark wasn't too fond of it. They were constantly having heated arguments considering she would regularly pick Vicky up and wouldn't bring her back home until early the next morning.

One day, my brother had his last straw and got fed up when she dropped her off and his wife was high as a kite.

He went over to Brenda sitting in her car and knocked her out cold. Of course, the next day I was at the jail bonding him out. I didn't get on to him for it; he knows I would have done the same. Being overprotective of our family is something to be proud of. After all, if it wasn't for them we'd have nothing, and we'd be nothing.

Following that morning, Brenda never showed back up at the house again. Either she learned a solid lesson or my brother hit her with a solid right that must have made her forget where he lived. He and Vicky began taking marriage counseling classes to try to salvage what was left of their relationship. They would drop Katie off at Mom's house and she'd watch her while they were gone. But I feel that the stress of Mom seeing her young boy constantly dealing with problems ended up taking its toll on her and it was too late. Our beautiful mother, who had always shown nothing but reckless love for us, passed away from a stroke not long after Mark and his wife fully reconciled. She died not knowing that in a few months she would have been a grandmother all over again after Archer was born.

The passing of our mother surely tested our sanity, but we did our best to hold it together for one another. Archie and Kate were keeping my brother preoccupied and that helped him focus on his family instead of finding a new way to drown the pain. I took up work at the shop to keep Dad company since I knew he was having a difficult time dealing with the loss of his wife of thirty years. But you know how the saying goes; that when it rains it pours, and it was raining cats and dogs.

The pain and loneliness were too much for Dad's heart to handle and it eventually gave way. He died of a heart attack not even a year after Mom left us and it had a devastating effect. I turned to alcohol for a brief but daily escape from what seemed was a never-ending nightmare of reality. And Mark, well, Mark completely lost it. It was the beginning of a hellish set of events that sent his life into a downward spiral.

My brother was affected the most by Dad's departure as he had developed a very strong bond with him working at the shop and all for a few years. He had turned to alcohol like me, but it appeared Vicky had a better idea to help his sorrow and ease his torment. She began hooking back up with Brenda and getting a hold of their drug of choice to get a quick high on, meth. According to her, she found Mark drunk and crying in his car in the driveway one night and that's when she introduced him to her magic stuff. At least that's what she told me when I confronted her about it. All it took was one time for the devil to get a good grip on him and I didn't recognize my little brother after that.

One afternoon, I randomly stopped by to check on my niece and nephew and to see if they were being kept well-dressed and well-fed. There was no answer to the knock on the door and it had been locked with the deadbolt. I could hear Archie crying inside so I didn't think twice about kicking the door open to see what was going on. I wasn't taking any chances, especially now that the kids' parents were the town's well-known drug addicts. When I got through the door and realized what was going on, I felt my face get searing hot and the veins in my arm felt a burning like I had been injected with boiling water. Archie was crawling around the living room naked with a syringe in his hand, which I quickly ran over to retrieve. Luckily, it didn't have a needle in it or I would have easily caught a case that day.

Vicky and Mark were passed out on the couch and

she still had a belt tightened around her left arm. I pulled her from the couch and threw her off the porch and onto the front lawn. My brother was next, except he got an ass-kicking as well. They knew why I did it because they didn't say a damn thing, and I think it was better that they didn't. I went back inside to get Archie and grabbed Kate who was sleeping in her bedroom. After picking up some of their toys and walking to my car I told Mark that I would be taking care of the kids until he could grow some balls and become a responsible father again. They were allowed to visit them anytime they wanted, but their new home was with me for the time being.

It wasn't until a few weeks later that I found out the lovely couple had gotten into some trouble with the law, and this time it was serious. In a desperate attempt to search for a way to not only fund their habit but also keep their house from being foreclosed on, they broke into a wealthy woman's home, a prominent figure in the community. The police found her tied, gagged, and half-conscious a few hours later after her daughter reported to the authorities that she couldn't get a hold of her.

Everyone knew who was most likely responsible for it even before the police made the arrests. I wasn't helping Mark anymore. I was done with it since I found out a worker had caught him stealing tools from the shop. I wasn't going to let him run Dad's business into the ground. It was all we had left of him. He needed to learn a lesson the hard way before he turned up dead soon.

I went through the courts to gain custody of his kids and since then I never stepped back inside of a bar. I took care of Archie and Kate like they were my own while their dad and mom were away. Their house was put up for rent during their incarceration and that earned just enough to cover the mortgage. He and Vicky did almost four and a half years for their crime and he cleaned himself up entirely after that. I can't say the same for her. She kept on with her habit, moved out of town and didn't come back, not even for a visit. I think it was for the best. If only she had stayed away.

I pulled into my driveway as darkness began to set in. The rain was coming down heavily now with no end in sight. I took a brief shower and lay down for the night, but with the endless twisting and turning and lightning constantly illuminating the room it was a struggle just to fall asleep. A feeling in my gut was telling me something wasn't right, but I just couldn't figure out what it was.

After what felt like an eternity of counting sheep I eventually managed to doze off.

CHAPTER TWO

Nice Catch

It had only been a few days since I had seen Kate and her brother, but I wanted to go around and surprise them by taking them a couple slices of their favorite pizza. It got pretty lonely not having them around as much anymore. We are meant to be social creatures, and, well, I just don't have a lot of people to socialize with around here, not that I'd have much to socialize about with them anyway. I can't say I have much patience for stupidity and with having too many acquaintances in my life there's a greater risk of someone testing my restraint.

Driving up to their house I could already see them through the living room window jumping up and down on the couch. I laughed at what looked to be their dad trying to get them to settle down. What a vibrant change compared to the times when there seemed to always be a dark cloud looming over the home. I liked it better this way, it was much more peaceful.

As I went to knock I noticed the door was showing a bit of damage. From the looks of it I'd say somebody had tried to break in. The footprints and splintered door frame were eerily reminiscent of the time I had broken in to a live scene from a drug intervention documentary.

"Who is it?" I covered the peep hole because who passes up that opportunity any chance they get?

"Your ex. You want some of this pie, baby?" If I hadn't chosen a mundane job I probably would have been a stand-up comedian.

"Hey kids, look what Uncle Eric brought!" He opened the box to show them and they clapped with excitement. Their smiles were bright and contagious.

"What do you say to Unky Eric?"

"Thank you, Unky Eric!" The perfectly synchronized voices echoed throughout the house.

"They actually just finished eating spaghetti, but these rascals have a bottomless pit in their stomachs. Somebody should have warned me about this. But thanks for dropping by and always thinking about the kids. I haven't had a bite myself 'cause I've been cleaning the reels since I got off work and getting everything else ready for tomorrow. You're going, right?"

"Yeah, I told you I'm always down to get on the water. Besides, work at the shop has slowed down and I'm only having one guy work Saturdays instead of the usual, so I'll be free. Paul's been tight with money and I'm letting him put in some extra hours."

"You're a good dude, Eric."

"Yeah, well, you know how Dad taught us."

"Amen to that, Brother." He sighed.

"Say, Bro"—I couldn't help being a little intrusive, but when it's family it's my business—"what happened to the door outside? I noticed a few marks on it like somebody was trying to come in."

"Yeah, last night, when I got home, I picked up the kids from next door and took them to get some nice clothes for Archie's party. Figured I'd get that out the way so I wouldn't be in a rush that day. Well, when we got back, my neighbor Steve met me at the fence and told me he had scared somebody off banging at the door and trying to get in a window. It was dark so he couldn't make out who it was. His wife had tried to call me, but you know how cell service is around here."

"That's for sure. What about his cameras? Didn't he have some around his house?" One of my favorite things aside from being a sarcastic asshole was playing detective.

"*Had* cameras before the rats chewed through the wires. Besides, I doubt they would have caught anything. Like I said, it was too dark and those things look like they're from the Civil War anyway. It would have been more frustrating trying to make out who the pixels were on screen than it was not having any video at all." He always had a valid point.

"All right, man. Don't keep your guard down."

"Never," he assured me. "Hey, so we're planning on heading out around nine tomorrow morning. You meeting us here?"

"I'll be here. Have a good one. Goodnight kids!"

"Goodnight Unky Eric!"

It was around ten thirty when we finally left Mark's house for the boat storage. You could count on him for almost anything, but punctuality was something you'd never find on one of his resumes.

"What's that munching noise? Do you have a mouse in the truck, Bro?" I turned to the back seat to see Archer and his sister having a field day with their bag of chips. They always laughed at my pitiful attempts at humor, and

I think that's what I liked best about them. "I hope you guys brought sunscreen."

"Where are we going?" I asked Mark as he made a left turn instead of the usual right we make at that particular intersection.

"I'm going to pick her up." The grin on his face could have stretched from sea to shining sea.

"All right, all right. I feel you," I told him, following it up with a quick fist bump. Being the third wheel was a passion of mine I had mastered years ago. But I wasn't complaining; the sense of freedom was an exhilarating high I had gotten addicted to, although not having someone to constantly argue with can get a little boring.

"I know it's a lot to ask, Eric, but please don't be stupid. And you know exactly what I'm talking about too."

I threw my hands in the air as if I didn't have a clue what he was referring to. But on the inside I knew precisely what he meant. "I haven't said a damn word, man."

"Well, I hope we can keep it that way for the rest of the day," he told me with a stern look.

Now, I love my brother to death and don't usually pass up an opportunity to humiliate him by acting a fool, but I was willing to give him a pass this time and make a respectable first impression of myself. The only exception to that was if he got the ball rolling first. Regardless, I decided I'd try to be a good boy and keep fairly quiet the rest of the trip.

"Just give me a minute." He hopped out of the truck and walked towards the front door of the house when we arrived. After a few minutes, along came the spider with a new prize inside of its web. A slender brunette with straight, long hair who could have easily been a runner-up in a Miss America pageant, or at the very least a part-time model, followed closely behind him. I honestly think she must have forgotten her glasses because you'd have to be legally blind to find any attractiveness in Mark.

He came up to my door and opened it. I sat there not moving for a moment, still in my seatbelt. "What? Oh shit, sorry!" I knew the drill, but I just like to make things a little difficult sometimes. I got out and hopped in the back seat with the kids.

After we were all inside he introduced everybody and we shook hands. "Angelica, this is my daughter, Kate, my son Archer, and my big child, I'm sorry, my big brother, Eric."

"Nice to meet you, Angelica." I turned back to my brother with a smirk, letting him know that the game he was playing with me was dangerous. Once you open the flood gates there is nothing left to do but drown.

"Daddy, is that your girlfriend?" Archie couldn't help his curiosity and we all know that children do a lot of learning through asking questions.

"Archer! She's a girl, yes. And she's my friend, yes."

"It's his girlfriend, I heard Daddy talking to her on the phone last night."

Thank you, Kate, for making this ride a little more entertaining. I see you're starting to take after your uncle.

"Katie, we do not listen to adult conversations while they're talking on the phone. You understand?"

"Yes sir," she replied and turned to me with her hand over her mouth to keep herself from laughing.

Seeing their dad moving on led me to believe they had a pretty good idea by now that their mother wasn't coming back. It had been a long time since either one of them had even asked about her. My brother didn't seem to care if the kids missed her or if they wanted her to return.

I don't blame him. They deserve a bright future, and if Angelica wanted to step up to the plate and give him a hand then more power to her.

After a quick pit stop for the toilet we made it to the boat storage and Mark signaled to me to help him attach his boat to the truck. I felt it somewhat odd because I usually get out to help anyway, so I imagined there was something on his mind. I walked into the storage where he pretended to be making himself busy fiddling with something.

"What's up?"

"Did you notice when I got on my phone at the gas station just a while ago?" he asked.

"Yeah, why? Who was it?"

"Vicky left me a voice message. She sounded—"

"Why am I not surprised that it had something to do with her now that I see you acting a little weird?" I have a bad habit of cutting people off, but my lack of patience beats me to the punch before I can make any rational decisions.

"She sounded a little psycho, and I don't think I've ever seen her act this way all the years I've known her."

"What about the time she threw Katie's cat in the bonfire when she was high?" I reminded him. "That wasn't psycho to you?" "What did she tell you?"

"She asked me how I was doing with my 'Barbie girlfriend' and if I thought my new girl would stick around after she found out about her."

Now I could understand why Mark was acting suspiciously. He had found a nice and beautiful girl willing to stick around and maybe help him raise his kids, and imagining all of that being washed down the drain in the blink of an eye by some piece of shit lowlife would put a knot in anyone's stomach.

"How did she even get your number? I bet it was Brenda, huh? I wouldn't doubt if Vicky has gotten her to follow you around to see who you're with or what you're up to. Don't ever underestimate those crackheads 'cause they'll pull a fast one on ya."

"I don't know, Bro. But she also told me that if I wasn't going to take her back then I could forget about me living a happy life without her. She said I should tell my new girl to always look over her shoulder. I don't know what to do, Eric. It almost makes me think I should slow things down with Angelica so that I don't put her in any danger."

"No! Screw that! Don't let that bring you down, you have to be stronger than that. If you let her instill fear in you then you're letting her win. She's going to have to accept that things aren't going back to the way they were. You have a lot ahead of you to lose sight of."

"A part of me feels like it would be the right thing to tell Angelica everything, but I'm really scared she'll be too afraid and cut things off with me. Anyway, I guess you're right. I shouldn't let this get to me. She always used to threaten me in the past just to get her way and never did a damn thing."

"I'll be damned if I'm going to let her ruin my fishing today, and you shouldn't let her either." I made it clear to him. "So look, just give yourself a couple of days to clear your head and then decide if you really want to tell Angelica about her. That would be the best thing to do. Now, go get in the truck and back it up so we can get out of here.

They're probably wondering what's taking us so long."

"Aye aye, captain!"

He hopped into his truck and I guided him as he reversed. I was already irritated by the things he had told me, but I wasn't going to let that spoil my fun. Right at that moment I just wanted to feel the breeze hitting my face and the comforting rock of the waves under my feet. We hooked up and were on our way.

It ended up being a beautiful afternoon on the lake. The fish were biting and the kids were thrilled to be out there. Angelica was helping the little ones with whatever they needed and it really looked like they enjoyed having her along. Mark thought he was a badass 'cause he was ahead of me on fish. One after another he was reeling them in.

"Oh yeah, baby! Here we go!" he yelled as he brought in what looked like a ten-pounder and held it up in front of him. Of course he turned towards me as I expected just to rub it in my face.

"I'm proud of you, man. That's a really nice catch. Oh, and that fish isn't so bad either," I told him. I quickly turned back around with a straight face before I could see their reaction.

I threw my line out. It was my turn to shine.

CHAPTER THREE

An Uninvited Visitor

I spent the greater part of Sunday afternoon driving from store to store in search of a good security camera for my brother's house since I figured he'd never do anything about it himself. Mark wasn't too inclined to take anyone's advice, so it was up to me to routinely make sure he was taken care of and staying out of trouble. Although I wasn't nearly as worried about him getting into any predicaments as was the case several years back, our new guest in town had aroused my protective instincts once again.

My phone rang just as I had narrowed down my choices to something I thought was the perfect pick. "Hey Bro, how's it going?" I answered.

"They came into the house, Eric." He sounded a little upset.

"What do you mean they came into the house? Who came into the house?"

"Somebody broke in when I took the kids out to lunch and they took a couple of things, including something very dear to me. But I think ... I think I know who it was."

Well, so much for the camera now, I thought to myself as I set it down and started making my way out to the car.

"Who, and what'd they take?"

"Remember the gun Dad gave me when I had just got the house so I could 'protect the family' like he said? It's gone. My fuckin' gun is gone, and I'm almost positive it was Vicky who did it."

Why was I not taken aback? It was starting to feel like every time I talked to him now she was becoming the topic of conversation.

"You have got to be kidding me! The Nineteen-eleven? You sure it's gone? Did you check every spot in the house? And how are you so sure it was her?" I was beginning to get more upset than he sounded to be, not only because it was our dad's old gun, but it was a hell of a pistol. Over the years he had gotten many offers on it, including some worth quite a penny, but he couldn't be persuaded to let it go. I didn't blame him one bit.

"I never move that gun, Eric! She's the only person who knew where I kept it all the time. It couldn't have been anyone else 'cause they also took some pictures of the kids off the fridge. They didn't even go through the rest of the house. She knew what she was coming in here for."

"What about the neighbors? Did you ask Steve if he had seen something this time?"

"Steve's not even home. Him and his wife left this mornin' and have been gone all day. That gun means a lot to me, even more so now with Dad not here. I'm gonna get it back one way or another."

"Look, as pissed as this makes me, I think you should probably just call the cops and file a report and do things the right way. They'll run into her sooner or—"

"Eric, you know damn well I can't call the cops, Bro! Have you forgotten that I'm not even supposed to have any guns around me?"

He was absolutely right about that. There wasn't really much we could do but get it back ourselves before she traded it off for a couple of hits to get high or did something stupid with it. Regardless, I wasn't going to let him do it on his own. Almost every single time I've let him try to take care of things by himself because of his stubbornness it has never ended well.

"All right, listen; let me know when you're planning on—"

"No, no, no! You listen! I got it, dude! Don't think I don't appreciate you trying to be there for me and help me all the time, but you gotta let me take care of some things on my own. Let me take care of the shit that I get myself into. OK?"

"Neither of us have to do this, Mark! I can hit up a couple of guys I know and they'll get it back. You don't need to get your hands dirty. Listen to me for fuck's sake!" I wasn't expecting him to budge. Usually, when he sets his mind on something that's pretty much it, but I figured it was worth a try.

"I'll give you a call when I get it back. I got this, man. You're always trying to save me from the world 'cause I'm your little brother. Stop trying to be a hero. Shit!"

I was beyond the point of trying to reason with him now and I was letting the situation get the best of me. "Why the fuck did you call me then! You think you don't have two kids waiting on you every day to get home! You're not in prison anymore so act like you give a shit about them!"

"Fuck you!" he yelled at me and dropped the call before I could respond.

"No, fuc—" I wasn't able to get it all out after realizing he was no longer there. I noticed a young couple in the parking lot staring at me while I sat in the car.

"The hell are y'all looking at!"

There was no use in being there anymore. I put my car in drive and made sure I let everyone around know I was making an exit. I didn't know where I was headed, but it wasn't home. I needed to clear my head. It had been quite a while since things had gotten that heated between the two of us.

The sun was all the way down when I made my way home from driving around town and stopping to shoot several games of pool at the local billiard hall. That was what would typically keep me out of trouble as a teenager. I don't know if I would necessarily consider myself a pool shark, but there have been plenty of times when I've cleared the table on some of the best players in the county. My brother and I would enter the tournaments on Monday nights several years ago. It wasn't unusual for a brawl to break out when the opposition didn't appreciate how quickly we'd send them back to their seats. Those were the simpler times and being there just revived a lot of old memories I wish I could relive.

I switched on the TV when I got in the house but quickly changed my mind when the local news began talking about another shooting nearby. I wasn't in the mood to get riled up again because of other people's stupidity so it went back off. There had been a recent rise in drug overdoses and violent crime around the Paloma area, which was surprising, it being a close-knit, rural community. You would sometimes get word about a break-in here and there, but for the most part everyone tended to mind their own business and keep their hands to themselves, that is until of late.

Mark was heavy on my mind and I began to wonder if he had gone out to look for Vicky and get his gun back or if maybe his temper had cooled down enough for him to make a more rational decision. I sat down at the kitchen table after grabbing a snack and decided to give him a call. Several hours had gone by since our shouting match so I figured enough time had passed that we could calmly talk about how to reasonably resolve the issue.

His phone rang several times until it eventually went to voicemail. I tried calling again and I just couldn't reach him. Was he still this upset that he kept ignoring my calls? I know I would irritate the hell out of him from time to time, but it was never to the point where we'd hold a grudge against each other. Things would normally calm down pretty quickly. Had he not entertained the idea of going out on his own to find his crazy ex-wife who was most likely armed it wouldn't have bothered me to just get in touch with him the following day. I had to go find out what was going on or else I might not be getting any sleep that night.

I grabbed my car keys and within half an hour I was driving by his house. His truck was not in the driveway and all of the lights were off inside. The next-door neighbors appeared to be home so I pulled in to ask them if they had seen him.

"Hey, how's it going, Eric? You here to pick up the kids?" Steve asked when he opened the door.

"The kids are here?"

"Oh, I thought that's why you were here. I'm sorry. What's going on? What can I do for you?"

"I have been trying to get a hold of Mark, but he's not

picking up his phone. So I wanted to ask if you had seen him."

"I've been calling him too and he doesn't answer me either. He dropped them off well over an hour ago and asked my wife if she could watch them 'cause he had to go run an errand alone. I gotta wake up early for work tomorrow, Eric, and I need him to get the kids so I can go to bed.

Now I was truly starting to worry. My brother wouldn't leave the kids next door this late knowing the neighbor had work the following day. By this time he would most likely be getting their stuff ready for the babysitter the next day and getting ready for bed himself.

"Steve, listen, it's very important I go and find Mark. I think he might have gotten into something 'cause you know he's usually home with the kids at this hour. Please tell your wife to watch them a little longer and I'll pay her for it. I promise."

"Well, all right. I'm going to bed, but she'll stay up. Just please don't be long."

"Hey Uncle Eric. Are you picking us up? Where's Dad?" Kate had heard us talking and came to the door.

"Hey, sweetie. Your dad got a flat tire on his way back home and I came to borrow some tools from Steve so I can go help him get it changed. We'll be right back shortly, don't worry." She nodded and I was away as fast as I could.

I had absolutely no idea where to begin because I couldn't think of a place Vicky could possibly be staying at that moment. I imagined maybe Brenda would be able to help me out, but I wasn't sure where to find her either. Even if I did find her, the last thing she'd do would be to give me any information about where I could locate her friend. Bribing her might get her to talk and I was willing to try anything just then. I headed towards the last few places I knew she would frequently hang out, but that was years ago.

Suddenly, I got a bright idea that might help me get some information from Brenda if I did get hold of her. I know another person who would be just as invested in finding my brother—Angelica. Brenda might feel less intimidated if I had a girl with me and be more willing to talk. I did a U-turn and headed towards her place keeping my fingers crossed that she would be home.

In no time at all I was knocking on her door. If Mark was all right and was just taking a bit longer than he expected, well, he was probably going to hate me for getting his girlfriend involved. Sooner or later she would have to find out one way or another. He would probably forgive me down the road easier than I would forgive myself if something happened to him. If he turned out to be fine, I thought this would be my sign to start minding my own business a little bit more and stay out of his.

"Hey, Eric. What brings you over here tonight?" She answered the door and looked around as if she was expecting someone else to be there with me. I didn't take it as a good sign. I knew precisely who she was looking for.

"Hey, I'm sorry for just showing up unexpectedly, but there's no other way I could reach you. Listen, I'm just going to be straight with you. I'm looking for my brother and I think he could've gotten himself into a bind. Have you talked to him lately?"

"No, well, not very recently. It's been maybe two or three hours. I did text him probably half an hour ago, but he never messaged me back. What kind of trouble is he in?"

"Do you think you can come with me and help me look for him? I'll tell you about it in the car. I just really need to make sure he's OK."

"Yeah, yeah, of course. Just give me a second." She went back inside.

Angelica not being in touch with him in the past few hours was even more concerning. If anyone would have known where he was or if something had happened to him I figured it'd be her; that is if they hadn't gotten into it also and were playing the silent game too.

"So what's going on?" she asked me in the car.

"Mark's ex-wife has been back in town and she's been threatening him. She doesn't like the fact that he's doing a lot better now and he has a girlfriend. Not sure how she found out about you, but we have an idea. That *idea* is who we have to go look for right now. She'll probably be able to tell us where the ex-wife is staying."

"Hold on, so why would Mark be with his ex if she's been threatening him?"

"Well, I'm not sure if he told you, but someone broke into his house earlier today. He says he's almost certain it was her and she took something very valuable to him. I think he went to get it back. I tried helping him, but we got into this huge argument about me always being in his business. So he wanted to go alone."

"How would I be of any help though, Eric?"

"His ex, Vicky, has a good friend named Brenda. She should know where Vicky is staying. If I find Brenda, she'll probably be too scared if I show up alone and won't give me any info. And if she still doesn't give me any info with you here, maybe you can make her talk better than I can without getting my hands on her."

Angelica stared at me wide-eyed most likely asking herself what on earth I was getting her into. I was afraid she would tell me to turn around and take her back home.

"Angelica, these are very bad people. Sometimes

this is the way you gotta play the game with them in order to get what you want. I'm sorry to get you into this, but I don't know of any other way to find my brother other than calling the cops. I just don't think they'll be of much help."

"I'll help you. I might look sweet and innocent, but I didn't grow up in the most loveliest of places. I learned to take care of myself pretty quickly growing up."

"Thank you so much, I really appreciate that."

"So what danger could he be in if it's his ex? Mark's a strong guy. Does she have a crazy boyfriend or something?" she asked.

"I don't know about that, but the thing is she stole his gun. And she's not in her senses most of the time. She hits the needle and the pipe pretty hard."

That didn't sit well with her. She focused directly ahead without saying a word. I could only imagine what was going through her head.

"He'll be fine. Maybe he did something stupid and got himself locked up." She finally broke the silence after several minutes trying to lift my spirits, and I assume hers as well.

"Yeah, you might be right. But I think by now he would have called someone to come bail him out."

My phone rang almost on cue.

"See, that's probably him." I liked her optimism, except I was a magnet for bad luck and it followed me everywhere I went.

"Eric, it's Steve. The cops just left my house and they were looking for you. They told me they went to your house and tried to call you, but apparently they have an old number, so I gave them your new one."

"Did they tell you what they wanted or say anything about Mark?" Another call started coming in. "Hey Steve, thanks a lot. I'm getting a call and it might be them. I'll talk to you later."

"Is this Eric, Mark Acosta's brother?" It was an unfamiliar voice.

"Yes, this is him. Who is this?"

"This is Detective Martinez with the Paloma Sheriff's Office. Your brother was involved in an incident and is in critical condition at University Medical. You have to get over th—" I hung up and suddenly felt a chilling cold take over my body and run into my stomach. I held on tightly to the steering wheel and stepped on the gas.

"What's going on? What happened!" Angelica was beginning to panic.

"It was a detective. Mark's in the hospital."

CHAPTER FOUR

If I Could Go Back in Time

The drive to the hospital was nothing but a blur of lights and sounds I couldn't distinguish, yet at the same time it felt like an eternity. We were quiet the whole way there, though I don't think there was anything we could have possibly said to describe what we were feeling. Just over a week ago everything had seemed so perfect. We had made it through what we felt were the worst times in our lives only to find ourselves once again in a hellish nightmare.

We ran into the emergency room looking to find information about my brother. I was trying to keep a positive attitude and be hopeful, but I was always the type of person to prepare myself for the worst. Or maybe it was simply a part of human nature.

"Yes sir? How can I help you?"

"I'm looking for Mark Acosta, I'm his brother and this is his wife. I was told that he's in critical condition and we need to go in and see him as soon as possible," I explained to the woman behind the counter.

"I'm sorry, but they're still trying to stabilize him at the moment. You'll have to wait until they say it's OK for you to go back there."

"What happened to him? What's wrong with him?"

"He came in with two gunshot wounds. That's pretty much all of the information I can give you right now. Just please have a seat and as soon as I hear from the doctors I will call you up."

"Ma'am, please go check again to see if we can go in," I pleaded. It was taking a lot of strength to keep from bolting through the doors and go looking for him. A couple of minutes longer and I don't think I would have been able to restrain myself.

Just as Angelica and I were making our way to the waiting area a doctor came through the emergency room doors.

"Is there family here for Mr. Acosta? Mark Acosta?" he asked the room.

"Yes! We're his family."

"Please come with me."

I couldn't tell by the expression on his face if I could breathe a sigh of relief or expect something dreadful. I'm usually very good at that, but I figured as much as these guys see in the ER on a daily basis they might be desensitized to it all by now.

The doctor led us down a hallway and we came to a stop just outside of a room.

"Mr. and Mrs. Acosta, your loved one has suffered extensive damage to some of his vital organs and we cannot stop his internal bleeding. It might be best if you begin to say your farewells. I'm sorry, there's just nothing else we can do for him." He put his hand on my shoulder and walked away. I could not believe what he had just finished telling me.

We slowly entered the room fearful of what we were about to see, and when I saw him, that is when reality truly set in. My baby brother lay there almost gracefully but with a tube in his mouth and IVs in both of his arms. Angelica burst into tears and I collapsed to my knees beside his bed. I reached up and held his hand.

"Mark ... brother ... I'm so sorry. Please forgive me. I tried everything to get to you, I promise. You gotta be strong and hang in there, for Archer and Kate. His birthday is coming up, come on, man! Let's go throw the football around, Bro." The tears were flowing down my cheek and I don't think I had ever felt so helpless and alone, not even when both of our parents passed.

I tried to hold on to whatever hope I had left in me, but from what the doctor had told us I knew the chances of him making it through this were nonexistent. I needed to be strong as well, if not for myself then for the kids. I completely broke down and laid my head by his side thinking about their precious faces when the time would come to tell them about their father.

After a few minutes the beat on the monitor became a single ominous tone. The nurses rushed in and we were ushered out of the room so they could work on him. I slammed my fist against the wall in the hallway trying to find a way to wake up from this dream. Why did this happen to him now? Why when he was getting his life together and on the right path taking care of his family? It's as if life knows when we're happy and it does whatever it can to take our happiness away because we are undeserving of it.

One of the nurses came out almost ten minutes later to give us the devastating news. "We're deeply sorry. If you would like to go in and spend some time with him now you may go ahead."

We went back in and this time he was all cleaned up. There were no more hoses and all of the machines were off.

All anyone would have thought was that he was getting a much-needed rest after a hard day at work.

"I'm so sorry for your loss, Eric." Angelica tried to console me, struggling to get any words out.

"*Our* loss. It's *our* loss, Angelica. He was a part of you just as much as he was a part of me. I could tell right away how happy you made him. I hadn't seen him that happy in such a long time."

"I'll help you with whatever arrangements you need to make for him. I know that's the last thing you want to deal with right now. You deserve some time to grieve."

I stood there beside him being a shaky mess and running my hand down his face. It's incredible how quickly things can change. I had never wished so much to be able to go back in time at least a single day. Hell, I wished I could go back even a few hours. There were so many things I would have done differently.

"Please don't think any of this is your fault. You did what you could." It was as if she knew what was running through my mind. "It's impossible to be looking after someone every minute of their life. You've been such a great brother to him, helping raise his kids, helping his life get back on track. He would always tell me how much you would go out of your way for him. I know it doesn't seem fair, and it's really not, but there are some things that are just out of our hands."

"The last time I talked to him we didn't quite say the nicest things to each other. I'm scared that I'm not going to be able to live that down," I said to her.

"Sometimes we say things we don't mean to one another in the heat of the moment. You were trying to do what you felt was right. You can't blame yourself for that." She tried to reason with me, but the pain I felt inside was too much for anything to make sense. I felt that no matter how things turned out, it was all my fault for not stopping this from happening.

There was a knock on the door and a nurse stuck her head inside.

"I'm sorry, Mr. Acosta, but there's someone out here who wants to have a word with you." She motioned for me to step out.

"I'm Detective Martinez, Eric. My condolences to you and your family. I'm very sorry about your loss. I knew your brother from back in the day. He was a really great guy."

"Yeah, you can say that again." I peered down at his badge. "So what happened, detective? Why is my brother lying dead in that room? Who did this to him?"

"That's why I'm here. It's very important that we get to the bottom of this as soon as possible. That way the person responsible for this can be brought to justice. I'd like for you and his wife, as I was told by the nurse, to accompany me to my office so I can ask you a few questions."

"That's just his girlfriend and she has absolutely nothing to do with this, so please leave her out of it. She had no clue about any of what was going on until a little earlier. Whatever you want to know you can get from me. I also have to make a quick phone call first to the person watching my niece and nephew to let him know what has happened."

"Yeah, yeah, of course. I'll give you some time to do whatever you need."

I stepped away to call Steve and let him know I wouldn't be picking up the kids until the next day. He was in complete shock and disbelief after hearing that my brother was gone. I made sure he wouldn't mention any of it to the kids. That grueling task was unfortunately going to come down to me.

I went to kiss my brother goodbye. I didn't want to leave him alone anymore, though I knew it was already too late. Had I not left him to fend for himself earlier that day none of this would have happened. But now I needed to focus on making sure the piece of shit who did this to him paid for what they did.

"Hey Angelica, I have to go meet this detective out here at the station and answer some questions. I'll drop you off at home so you can get some rest. The next couple of days are going to be pretty rough."

"What about all of the—"

"Don't worry about any of the arrangements right now. I'll come back tomorrow and take care of everything. I spoke with the staff and they said that was fine."

She went to my brother's side. It was all too surreal watching her cry over him. My eyes and ears were taking everything in, but I felt disassociated from reality. None of this was going to set in anytime soon until I walked into his empty house once again. It would be déjà vu all over, except this time it was permanent. He was never going to walk through that door.

We tried so hard to keep our composure as we walked away from him and left the hospital.

"Eric, what can you tell me about your brother's relationship with his ex-wife?"

"There was no relationship with his ex. That ended a long time ago." I stared down at my cup of coffee as I answered the detective's questions, all the while trying to balance the feelings of sorrow and hate that were battling with each other for dominance.

"Did your brother ever say anything about wanting to hurt Vicky? Did he hold a grudge against her for anything in the past?"

"Do you mean did Vicky ever say anything about hurting my brother? Why isn't that the question? Because that's exactly what happened."

"So she threatened him? Why?"

"Well, 'cause she's a crazy bitch who spends the majority of the day tweaked out on meth. She didn't like that my brother had recently rejected her. He was doing so good and moving on with his life. He had started dating Angelica not long ago, the girl who was with me at the hospital, and I guess Vicky just wasn't about to see them be happy together."

"Well, if he was doing so good now, why would he go looking for her and get himself into any trouble? All of this over some threats?" He leaned back in his chair and put his hands behind his head. I had a feeling that there was something more to the story that he wasn't telling me.

"What you really should be doing is getting Vicky out of jail and bringing her here and asking her why the hell she killed my brother. I figured that's the first thing you would have done."

"Eric, Vicky hasn't been arrested. We questioned her when we arrived on scene, but that was pretty much all we could do."

"Are you kidding me right now?" I stood up from my chair. "Mark is lying dead in a hospital bed and you're sitting here telling me that you haven't arrested her! Was it someone else who shot him! Is that it? That has to be it!"

"Please sit down and hear me out, Eric. The investigation is still ongoing so I can't give you many details. Like I mentioned to you before, I've known your brother to be a great guy, so this has caught me off guard as well. And I promise you I'm going to look into this as extensively as I can. I just need you to tell me everything you know, because truthfully this is starting to look like self-defense."

"Bullshit! My bro wouldn't fuckin' ruin his entire life over a gun. He wouldn't do that to his kids."

"What do you mean over a gun?"

"Look, someone broke into his house and stole a gun our dad had given him a long time ago. It was one of his most prized possessions. He was certain it was Vicky and we got into a huge argument because he wanted to get it back but wouldn't let me help him. If I would have stopped him, I'm sure he would still be alive."

"Why didn't you just call the cops and file a report?"

"Really? So you can arrest him for a felon having a firearm in his home? Come on, man. You know his history. It was your department that locked him up several years back. Or did you already forget?"

"Eric, I really want to believe you, I really do. And I'm trying to make sense of all of this. But we found him *inside* of her apartment and she had lacerations on her head. What kind of gun did your brother own?"

"It was a Colt Nineteen-eleven."

"We found that in his hand. He wasn't shot with that gun from what we can see, Eric. She had her own."

"I guarantee you she set him up! Yeah, she might be a tweaker, but don't ever underestimate them. Come on, detective, you gotta do your job a little bit better than this. Or try putting someone else on the case if it's something out of your range of experience."

"I know you're upset and it's hard to accept these

things about Mark, but no matter what happens I'm going to take everything you've told me into consideration and do the best I can to get to the bottom of this."

"Yeah, well, I hope that happens pretty quickly. If I catch her on the streets you're going to find her with more than just lacerations. Your best forensics guy won't be able to tell what the hell he's looking at."

"Eric, I know you used to have custody of his kids when he was in prison, so please think about them. Don't do anything stupid. They need you now more than ever."

He was right. No matter how badly I wanted to put Vicky in the ground just then, I had to think about Kate and Archer first. They were waiting for me. My heart sank once again just picturing their innocent faces.

"I'm done answering questions. My niece and nephew are waiting for me." I got up and he opened the door to the interrogation room.

"No matter how things are looking right now, I give you my word that I'll get to the bottom of it. I won't leave a stone unturned."

"Thank you, detective." I shook his hand and made my way out.

CHAPTER FIVE

The Bell Tolls for Thee

The day had arrived to lay my brother down into his final resting place. He would now be keeping Mom and Dad company and knowing they'd be together once again brought me some sort of comfort. The past couple of days had been an incessant wave of pain and suffering. I had no idea where I found the strength to tell my loving niece and nephew about their daddy, but it had to have come from somewhere else, because I don't believe I did it all on my own. Archie had been crying for days and Katie struggled to sleep as a result of her repeating nightmares. It hurt to even think about what had been running through their minds lately, but I could only imagine. Personally, what gave me nightmares was the look on their innocent faces the moment they found out.

Another thing which required an immense amount of strength was the restraint I needed not to hit the streets in search of Vicky. I'm positive most of my remaining energy came from the kids. I had an obligation to be there for them and getting in trouble by avenging my brother's death was the worst thing I could do to them. It wouldn't be fair. There was no other kin in the state to care for them as the few family members attending the burial had flown in from hundreds of miles. The very minimum I could do for Mark was make sure Archer and Kate were very well taken care of. I didn't let him down in the past when he was in prison, and I wasn't planning on doing it now.

The little ones were ready, dressed in their best attire, and I had spiffied myself up as well. We headed towards the funeral home where Angelica would be meeting up with us. I don't know if I had ever been more anxious in my life. Deep down I wanted to turn around and avoid the whole thing entirely because I knew that watching my brother being lowered into the ground would break me in two.

It felt like it was just yesterday when I was watching the same thing happen to my parents. There was a complex internal struggle within me trying to make sense of how any of it was fair. I realized that what kept me going aside from the kids was the little bit of hope I was holding on to that things would get better. I was looking forward to those days, and I was looking forward to Vicky never seeing another day of freedom in her life.

When we arrived at the service, I noticed the vast amount of people in attendance who were there to pay their respects. It was heartwarming seeing everyone there for him and I just know it reflected on the kind of person he was. Whether it was from a long-lasting friendship or a short time sharing a few beers with strangers, he had his way of leaving an impression on people. I'm sure many of them knew about his prior struggles with addiction and his bad choices because of it, but in the end it was his heart of gold that defined him.

"I'm so sorry for your loss." Uncle Ron gave me a hug as I walked to the front towards the casket.

"Thank you, Uncle. I'm glad you were able to make it. It's unfortunate that we must see each other again so soon under the same circumstances."

"It is, son. But we gotta keep our heads up and move forward, not necessarily for ourselves but for the ones who depend on us."

Truer words could not have been spoken. I was slowly coming to terms with accepting the fact that we must let go of our hate no matter how strong it is because it destroys us more than the people responsible for causing us to have that hate in the first place.

I escorted Archer and Kate to the first pew where Angelica was sitting and they ran to be by her side. It was as if they could sense my brother's love in her and it amazed me how quickly they had seemingly become attached.

I approached the casket and upon seeing his face I could instantly picture in my head a lot of the moments we spent playing together as kids. All of those years of happiness and sorrow we shared with each other would never have led me to believe I would one day be saying goodbye to him like that. I tried so hard to hold my composure and be strong in front of the kids, but a person can only hold in so much before everything rips loose.

Slowly making my way to the podium made me feel so alone for some strange reason. It brought back memories of my parents yelling out, "You can do this!" when they tried to encourage me at a school function where I had to give a speech. This time there was only silence. I felt like a lost fawn looking for its mother, its father, and now its brother for some sort of consolation and support, but they were all gone.

"I'd like ... I'd like to thank everyone for being here today for Mark. It's very moving to see so many of you here to share this very intimate moment and it allows us to see just how outgoing and friendly my brother was towards people. And I'd like to apologize as well if I ramble since I don't have anything prepared in advance that I wanted to say. Maybe my words to him can pretty much sum up what I feel, what he meant to me, and how I'll always remember him.

"Ever since you came into this world, Brother, I took on the role of 'protector'. I don't know if it was something I wanted or chose to do at that moment, but it felt like it came so naturally. I was so little myself with such a huge responsibility that I felt like a superhero taking care of you and making sure you were always safe. But not only were you my sibling growing up, you were also my sidekick. We played together, got into trouble together, and even fought with each other, yet we both knew that nothing could ever break the bond we had. I carried you home when you fell off of your bike and broke your ankle, and I took the blame when you broke Dad's back window on his truck. And I would do anything that ever got you and me in trouble all over again because the things we sowed yesterday are the invaluable memories we reap today.

"I watched you grow up into a man and create two beautiful children, a responsibility I haven't even taken on myself to this day. And I also watched you live some of your darkest moments after Mom and Dad passed away. Many of us here are witnesses to the battles you overcame, and I personally saw the hell you lived that nobody else knew about. And not even that held you down. I might have felt like your superhero back then, but you were the one with superhuman strength. Show me where you found that strength, or how you came to have it, because I'm the one who needs it now.

"They say things happen for a reason and sometimes we won't know why they do until the right time comes. Well, I think we all know the precise reason why most of these things happen and that is because evil beings exist in this world. You're not gone because this place was too much for you. You're not gone because you weren't strong enough, 'cause you proved every person wrong who thought you weren't. You're gone for the simple fact that you shined so bright that it blinded those afraid of the light. You were all they saw when they opened their eyes in the morning and until they closed them for bed. That was too much for them because you escaped their reign of darkness and were no longer a prisoner of their misery. You're gone because you were doing things right, and in a world of unrighteousness that is sometimes the price we must pay.

"Kate and Archer will be just fine. They are my children now. There won't be a single time when you'll look down and not feel proud of them. From now and beyond the moment they graduate high school, go to college, and create a family of their own, I will love and support them with as much commitment as I have to see you once again someday. I'll be talking to you every time I wake up and at every prayer before I lie down to sleep. Rest easy now, I'll take things from here. I love you, Brother."

I sat down between the kids and put an arm around them to hold them tight. We then reminisced on Mark's life as some of our friends and family said a few words from their time knowing him. And it wasn't long before we found ourselves at the cemetery saying our final goodbyes to my best friend who kept me company all those years.

Watching his casket descending into the ground felt like a tremendous weight crushing me more and more with every inch it was lowered. I felt nauseous and dehydrated, probably from the constant flow of tears running down my face. Katie was hysterical and Angelica did her best to comfort her.

I walked over to the grave and picked up a handful of dirt. "Tell Ma and Pop I miss them. You guys keep each other company now and keep an eye on us from time to time. I'll see you guys later."

I grabbed the kids to leave, hoping that after I left all of this behind my life would somehow slowly begin to return to normal somewhat. I knew deep down inside that it would more than likely take years for that to start happening, but it was fine with me. I'd already accepted from some of my past tribulations that healing comes as slow or as fast as you're willing to move on.

On our way to the parking lot I noticed a familiar face waiting for me. By the looks of it I don't think he had any good news, as if this day could have gotten any worse.

"Angelica, can you please take Katie and Archer to the car and wait for me there?"

"Yeah, sure thing."

"How are things going, detective?" I extended my arm out to shake his hand.

"Eric..." He paused for a second. "Eric, the district attorney took the case to a grand jury.... I'm sorry, but they decided to no-bill Vicky. They didn't think there was enough evidence to charge her with your brother's death."

"This has to be a joke! How incompetent does somebody have to be to serve as a juror here? What did they miss, because they must have missed something, right?"

"Eric, we, along with our forensics team, did everything we could. We presented all of the evidence we found and from the knowledge we gathered it shows that Mark was the aggressor in this case. His fingerprints were the only ones on that gun."

I couldn't help but smile at the absurdity I was hearing. "You mean to tell me that you guys and everyone on that jury were outsmarted by a drug-addict who probably has trouble tying her own shoes now because of how fried her brain is? Detective Martinez, I don't know what your record is on solving cases, or how many times you've gotten it wrong, but please don't let this be the one that taints your reputation for letting a murderer get off scot-free."

"There's nothing else I or the district attorney can do once the grand jury makes their decision. It's out of my hands, Eric. I can't change the facts of what happened. The investigation is closed."

"Do you know how many innocent people are in prison right now? Do you know that there are also guilty people running around without a care in the world because someone at some point fucked up? I know the system isn't perfect, so all I want is for you to please keep an eye out. You say you knew my brother from back in the day, but I knew him every minute of his life. I know he didn't go looking to hurt her, much less kill her. He had way too much to lose. And quite frankly neither you nor anyone else has to believe me, but let it rest on your conscience."

"You're right, we get things wrong from time to time and, trust me, I always go home and pray that I didn't screw something up. I want to see justice done just as anybody else."

"Just give me your word that if anything comes up you'll follow up on it. That's all I want."

"If I come across any little thing that raises my suspicion on this case, I give you my word that I'll look into it." He reached out and we shook hands once again.

I wasn't sure if I should even get my hopes up that anything would change and I'd get to see Vicky pay for what she did. But even the smallest bit of hope had been keeping me going the past several days. It's an incredible thing to have, because it's like a tiny seed you hold on to when you've lost it all and have nothing left in your life. You plant it and watch it grow like a new beginning ready to give new fruits. And right now I was holding on to my seed.

"I'll keep in touch with you, detective, and even though I don't like how things have turned out, thank you for the work you've done."

"I won't forget, I promise," he assured me.

Angelica gave the kids one last hug before we left the cemetery. All I wanted now was to be home with them and have a couple of slices of pizza and put on a movie to help ease their minds. It had been one hell of a day and I couldn't remember the last time I felt so exhausted. But this wasn't only physical exhaustion; I was mentally and emotionally drained.

"Listen, Angelica, thank you so much for everything you've done for us this week. Even though you really haven't known us for long you've treated us like family. Mark would have truly appreciated that 'cause I know I do. You're welcome to stop by any time you'd like to say hi to the kids and now that I'll be going back to run the shop next week I might need a sitter to watch them until they start school again. Think about it and let me know."

"It's been my pleasure. It's the least I could do for your brother. He was always so wonderful with me and returning the favor towards you guys makes me feel like I'm giving back a part of what he gave to me. And I'll think about your offer, Eric, thank you."

Archer didn't want to let her go, but as much as it pained me to see them hurt the way they did, we got into our vehicles and went our separate ways.

CHAPTER SIX

The Unexpected Encounter

The leaves, with their seasoned array of brown, orange, and yellow, had gracefully begun falling from the trees and the cooler autumn air was finally here. Kate and Archer were now back in school and I'd been keeping busy with work at the shop. Things appeared to be slowly easing their way back to some sort of normalcy, but it hadn't come quite so simply. In the past couple of months since Mark left us I'd had to find a counselor to help Kate deal with her dad's passing. She'd experienced issues adjusting herself to her new classes and I'd been told that she could possibly be suffering from anxiety. Fortunately, we had been seeing quite a lot of improvement and I wasn't surprised at all, I knew she was a strong girl.

Archer decided that he did not want a birthday party after all without my brother being there and I perfectly understood why he chose not to. I only prayed that as time went by everything that fell apart that day could slowly be pieced and sewn back together. I knew that's what Mark would have wanted and I made it my goal to make sure it happened.

Angelica found a full-time job at a hair salon so she wasn't able to watch the kids when I had to stay late for work. But she did spend time with them on the weekend and came by every once in a while to see how they were doing. I think having someone to check on our sanity from time to time definitely made things a little easier. It made me wonder if maybe I should start making plans to find a partner to keep me company. I knew I could do things on my own, but I would be more at ease with my niece and nephew having somebody there more permanently. Now I could fully comprehend how Mark felt when he was talking to me about this at the park a few months back.

It was a chilly Saturday afternoon and my stomach was rumbling from not having eaten anything all day. I headed over to the diner to grab a bite to eat now that I had finished running my errands. My two little rascals were at Angelica's house where I had dropped them off in the morning since they had a fun day planned filled with activities like painting and watching movies. What I wouldn't give to be a kid all over again.

When I arrived, it wasn't surprising that the place was packed to the gills. I personally blamed their chicken fried steak for giving it its five-star reputation. The restaurant was small and welcoming, something around the likes of what you'd see in an eighties movie featuring a rural town in the Northeast. Nonetheless, my reason for frequenting this eatery went a little far beyond the food itself.

"Hey Eric, what can I get for you today?" Carol always greeted me with a smile every time I sat down at the bar. She had seen me at my best and had to cut me off from ordering any more drinks at my worst. This is the typical small community where your local waitresses sometimes know more about you than your wife or girlfriend.

"Get me a lemonade, please, and I'll have the special for the day. And hopefully there's not a long wait 'cause I'm starving."

"You're still not drinking, huh?" she asked.

"No ma'am. But I've spent so much time at this bar that it feels a little nostalgic sitting up here from the better days. Plus, tables and booths aren't really my thing, unless I have some company with me."

"I hear ya. Well, that's good, and I'm really glad you've hung in there. Not many people are that strong-willed. And besides, the way you were going it was only a matter of time before you got yourself into trouble."

"Amen to that.... So what time do you get off today? Maybe we can hang out later and go shoot some darts or something."

"You know, that's actually not a bad idea, except I'm getting together with a few friends after work and we'll be having a couple of drinks at the pub. I mean you're welcome to come if you'd like, I'm sure they won't mind."

I figured asking her out was worth a shot seeing how I didn't have anything planned for the rest of the day. But I was never the type to get into a position where I felt like I was being intrusive, so I had to pass on this one.

"No, no, it's fine," I said. "If you're free next weekend maybe we can get together and do something then."

"I think that sounds like an even better idea," she replied.

Hang in there kids, Uncle Eric is working on it. It's just a matter of time, I thought to myself and accidentally let out a chuckle.

"What's so funny?"

"Oh, I, uh ... remembered something funny that happened earlier." It felt as if somebody had suddenly turned up the heat inside.

She was pouring me a glass of lemonade when I felt someone approach and sit at the stool beside me. I couldn't help but notice the look on her face as she glanced over at my new neighbor. Carol turned towards me almost in shock and then walked away.

"Hey Eric. She's really pretty, isn't she? By the way, I never got to tell you this, but I'm very sorry about your brother Mark. I never meant for anything to happen to him." The voice was all too unmistakable. I could sense her evil presence before she even said a word. It was Satan himself.

"You must not be in all of your senses, Vicky, or have lost the sense of fear to be coming up to me and mentioning my brother's name. If you know what's best for you, I suggest you stay away from me and move on with your life like I'm trying to do." I had taken a long hiatus from my unpredictable temperament to focus more on peace and tranquility, but I could feel a reemergence suddenly happening within me.

"Why is everyone always looking at me to be the bad guy? They weren't there, they don't know what happened. I was only defending myself." She took a cigarette out and went to light it.

"Ah, ah! No smoking in here! Take it outside!" Carol yelled at her from the other side of the diner. Everybody in town knew there was more to it than what Vicky was proclaiming. Nobody believed her and they all wanted to see her rot in prison almost as much as I did.

"You have some huge balls to be opening your mouth and saying what you're saying. I knew my brother a lot more than you did and I know you killed him in cold blood. I'm not going to rest until you're locked up and never see an ounce of freedom again. Now, I suggest you start making your way out of here or I might catch a case driving this fork into your throat."

"Don't threaten me, Eric. I'm always one step ahead." She began to slowly walk away, whispering under her breath, "I got away with it once and I can get away with it again. I'll make you beg for your life just like your brother did."

I jumped off of my stool and reached for her arm, yanking her back so hard that her phone flew out of her hand and shattered on the floor. "The next time I see you, they'll be taking you away in handcuffs so you can spend the rest of your miserable life where you belong. You're lucky I actually have something to lose or you'd be eating through a straw and shitting in a colostomy bag when I got done with you. Now get the fuck out of here before I actually lose my temper."

She picked up her phone and walked out of the door. I sat back down and the rest of the patrons resumed their conversations as if nothing had ever happened. Hell, if I would have killed her right then and there everybody would have probably told the cops they didn't see a damn thing. It still amazed me how forgiving they all had been towards my brother and the love I'd felt was beyond words. I must have run across every person from town twice by then who attended Mark's funeral since we buried him.

Carol came out of the kitchen with my food, but I had suddenly lost my appetite. My hands were shaking and my breathing was a bit faster than normal. But this wasn't from fear or intimidation, it was partly from a build-up of anger I'd carried for months ever since that fateful night. And the other part was from realizing how close I was to altering my life altogether had I acted on impulse.

"I'm gonna have to get that order to go 'cause I'm just not feeling it anymore, I'm sorry. If you only knew how close I came to—"

"Listen, don't let her get the best of ya, hun. She'll get hers when the time is right, I promise. There's no need to get all worked up about it. If you allow her to make you miserable then you're letting her win. Don't you ever forget that."

Everything she was telling me was absolutely right, and it reminded me of the time I had told Mark the same thing. But that made no difference to me just then, though she spoke nothing but the truth. It gets tiring holding it together for so long and essentially pretending to be someone you're not. I needed to clear my mind and relax. I wanted to remember what it was like to feel completely normal again before it all changed and my life became a struggle between being a role model and letting the beast inside of me loose. Whether we would like to admit it or not, we all have our breaking point and if you think you don't, well, you just haven't been tested enough.

I had made up my mind and tried not to entertain the thought of it anymore before I started to soften up and regret it. "I'll still take that box," I said to Carol. "And go ahead and pour me a shot of whiskey while I'm here."

CHAPTER SEVEN

An Offer You Can't Refuse

I woke up in my room the following morning with a pounding headache not remembering how I managed to get home or what exactly had occurred at the diner after my memory decided to take the rest of the day off. My phone alerted me to a low battery so I picked it up to put on the charger realizing that I had several missed calls from Angelica. *Shit! I was supposed to pick up the kids last night. I should have just listened to Carol. I'm such an idiot.*

Scolding myself wasn't going to do me any good now. I felt disappointed and ashamed for allowing the situation to get the best of me the day before, or maybe it was a side effect of the grueling hangover eating me alive from the inside. Regardless, I had to regain my strength and check up on Kate and Archer so I picked up the phone to make the call.

"Eric, are you OK? I called you several times last night, but you never answered."

"Look, I apologize, Angelica, I'm truly sorry. I know I was supposed to pick them up but apparently had way too many drinks and I pretty much lost track of everything. I honestly wasn't planning on it."

"You should have sent a text to ease my stress. I

still become a nervous wreck from time to time because of everything that's happened. I get really worried knowing you're all the kids have left."

"I understand and, again, I'm sorry. I ran into Vicky last night at the diner and things got a little heated. I was close to doing something stupid so I played it safe by downing a few shots instead. Trust me, I regret every second of it now."

"What did she say to you?" she asked.

"I'd rather not get into that. But I'll tell you this, it left me no doubt that my brother was not at fault for what happened to him, not that I had any doubt to begin with."

I might not remember anything after about the eighth shot, but one thing fresh on my mind was every single word she uttered to me as she walked away. I wasn't going to forget that so easily and I sure as hell wasn't going to back down on finding justice for Mark. She had awoken a darker side of me I had always feared would come out one day, and what better time to showcase what I was capable of than now?

"Well, we'll be here when you're ready. They just finished eating breakfast and are watching cartoons in the living room."

"Thank you so much. I'll be there within the hour, and please let me know what I owe you for keeping them overnight. I hope I didn't ruin any plans you had."

"No, don't worry about it. It's fine. We had a good time. I'll see you when you get here."

I felt my head throbbing as I stood up to jump into the shower putting my hand on the bed to keep from falling over. Just then a text message popped up on my phone. It was Carol. *Good morning, sunshine. Hope you're feeling good. You prob shouldn't have had all those drinks on an empty stomach. Got some friends to drop you off and take your car home. Ttyl.* If that's not top-of-the-line hospitality, I don't know what is. I didn't know if I should message her back. A part of me was too embarrassed and ashamed to reply, but then again she's mopped my vomit off of the floor in the past, so showing some gratitude was the least I could do. *Thank you, darling. Not doing that again.*

After a quick shower and forcing myself to hold down a full meal I started to gather my thoughts on what I had in store for Vicky. My mind was set and the constant nausea from the hangover helped fuel the spite I felt for her that much more. I was not going to be outsmarted by this vagrant wandering around without a care in the world thinking she had gotten the best of my brother and me. I was willing to put it all on the line now and show her precisely who she was dealing with. When it comes to love, I can give whatever I have unconditionally and not demand the same in return. But taking from me what I cherish most and mocking the pain I've suffered turns me into a ruthless monster that stops at nothing until the vengeance is mine.

I remembered her phone falling on the floor in the diner and I knew who I needed to get in touch with. This guy was a real character who I could confide in to take anything we ever talked about to the grave. We used to get into some very risky predicaments together when we were younger and it was only by the grace of God that we both became productive members of society. Hopefully he wasn't too busy to answer my call and give me a hand.

"Hello? Hello? Who's this? Greg?" He wasn't the brightest fellow, but his loyalty was unmatched.

"Hey Carlos, it's me, Eric. How you been?"

"Oh, shit! What's up, Eric! I've been good! You? Damn, dude, I haven't heard from you in a minute! I thought you were Greg, that asshole owes me money. Have you seen him by the way?"

"I've been hanging in there, just taking it a day at a time, you know? And no, I haven't seen Greg, but I'll let you know if I do."

"I'm sorry about your bro, man! He was a cool cat. That's very tragic what happened. Sorry I couldn't make it to his funeral; I was outta town but heard all about it."

"It's fine, don't even worry. But listen, I'm calling you 'cause I need a huge favor and I know I can count on you, like back in the day. Remember? Everything has to stay on the down low."

"Oh yeah, yeah, yeah, dude. Whatever you need, I gotchu! You know me, I ain't no punk."

That was music to my ears. Treating people the right way can not only help you create a lifelong friendship, it can also provide a trustworthy accomplice if the need ever arises.

"You're still working at the cellphone place, right?"

"Yeah, yeah, I'm still selling phones. Why? You need one? I just got the latest one, man. It has a nice camera and takes—"

"Listen to me, Carlos, I want you to find Victoria Acosta's number in the system and give her a call. She's probably desperate for a new phone right now."

"Oh that crackhead? I think she stole a phone from me once. What you got planned?"

"I don't want to get into any details, I just want her to get a new phone. Call her and offer her the best deal you can think of. I'll pay you for it myself, and I'll give you something extra for helping me out. Now, I need you to do this as soon as you can and let me know the moment she picks it up. And most importantly, make sure she keeps the same number and don't tell her the phone is free. I don't want her to get suspicious."

"That it? I can get that done quick. I just gotta keep an eye on her when she comes into my store though. Never know with these bums. You turn your back on them for a second and when you look again the front door's missing. Know what I mean?"

"I also want you to get me her friend Brenda's number. I gotta have a word with her. The last time I wanted to get a hold of her I had no idea where to start. And one last thing, do you know if Lester is still hustling with his side job?"

"Yeah for sure, man. I'll text you Brenda's number in a bit. And that boy Lester's still doin' his thing. You can catch him Tuesday nights at Billy Billiards in Tasco playin' the tourneys. It's a long-ass drive, but you'll find him. You not lookin' to get some of his shit for yourself, are ya?"

"I have a friend in dire need of something and he's got the best stuff in the state," I told him. "I saw too much of what Mark went through to even touch that. But that's about it, so let me know when the deal goes through and I'll send you some cash."

"All right, cool, cool. You got it, boss. I don't know what you're up to, but I like it! Ha ha! Take it easy, bro!"

Carlos sent me Brenda's digits, which was going to be the easier step of the next couple of things I had lined up. Getting her to actually give me what I wanted was going to take a little bit more work, but that's where Lester would come into play. Regardless, one way or another she was going to cooperate seeing how at some point in the past she had a role in the way everything turned out.

I called the number but after only two rings it went to voicemail letting me know she must have rejected the call. A tweeker's paranoia typically goes into overdrive the moment they realize someone unfamiliar must be looking for them. Thankfully, six calls later I managed to irritate her enough and she answered.

"Who the hell is this? Can you stop calling my phone, I'm a little occupied!" That wasn't the greeting I was expecting, but it was without a doubt better than nothing.

"Brenda, don't hang up, this is Eric."

"Eric? Mark's brother? How'd you get my number and why you callin' me?"

"I got it from a friend, but please hear me out. I need your help and I can make it worth your while like you wouldn't believe."

"Help? With what? Look, I had nothing to do with what happened to your brother."

"I know you didn't. You're not in any kind of trouble, I promise. All I want is for you to talk to Vicky and I can get you some of the best crank you've ever gotten your hands on. It will take you beyond the clouds, trust me."

"Vicky's a good friend of mine and I don't think I can do that to 'er." I had a feeling she would go that route, but drug fiends will turn on their own mothers just for a rock. That is one thing I'd bet my life on.

"I want you to give what I have for you a little taste, Brenda. Then once you talk to her, I'll double the amount. Don't pass up this opportunity. It's all just one simple phone call away. And if you're not willing to do it I can just as easily find somebody else, but you'll be beating yourself up for it later."

"So what all you want me to say to her?" That question was the sound of the ball bouncing into my court. And everybody was going to play by my rules.

"We'll meet up in a couple of days so I can give you the down payment and I'll explain everything to you then. Now, if she finds out that you and I talked I'm backing down from this altogether, and I'm not going to be too happy. I'm trusting you." Trusting a person like her is equivalent to trusting a speeding train to stop on a dime. But sometimes it doesn't hurt to make them think they're still somewhat dependable. You have to give them the illusion of being an important piece of the puzzle even when they don't have a clue what's going on around them. It decreases your chances of getting stabbed in the back just slightly.

"I ain't gonna say a thing to her. You got my word on that." She'd tell me anything in order to get a quick fix, but I was willing to take the gamble.

"And save my number so you'll know it's me and pick up," I told her. I don't think I necessarily needed to remind her of that. If she wasn't calling me to check up on our future rendezvous every few hours I'd start getting a little worried then.

I let Angelica know I was on my way to pick up the kids. Telling her about my plans might not be such a great idea at that moment. I didn't want her to get worried and think I'd end up six feet under like my brother, although I wasn't ruling out that possibility.

It was a quarter till eight Tuesday evening when I

entered the Tasco city limits in search of Lester. The first tournament would be starting soon and I didn't want to upset him by catching him at a bad time, especially if he ended up losing that night. That would decrease my chances of getting what I came for. The last time we hung out was approximately four years ago when he beat me three games in a row in the last pool tourney I played. The guy was a real pool shark. That demoralizing loss was a major reason I had not picked up another cue stick in years.

Aside from his pool skills, nobody could argue the fact that he was good at hustling outside of the pool hall as well. This wasn't your ordinary street vendor selling dime bags out of his Lincoln Continental. The word from many of my contacts was he had direct involvement with the Mexicans bringing shipments across the border. Of course, anyone who was wise enough never questioned him about it and to be honest I don't think they could have cared less. I only hoped he didn't get the suspicion I was some sort of informant looking to get something incriminating out of him. It wasn't out of the ordinary for an old acquaintance to turn snitch after disappearing from the radar for a while.

My phone went off pulling into Billy's and it was a welcoming message from Carlos I had eagerly been waiting for: *Vick picked up and activated phone, didn't ask questions*. Things were slowly looking up. Now all I had to do was pray she didn't take it to the nearest pawn shop.

I walked in and scanned for Lester, spotting him at the bar having a drink. As I made my way there he landed eyes on me and recognized me right away.

"Well, well, well ... it took you all these years to finally gain some courage and come get your rematch, huh?" His firm handshake was his personal signature meaning he meant business.

"I've been waiting all this time in hopes that you've become a little rusty in your game. Now I'm here to take back what's mine," I joked with him.

"Hell, good luck with that! But let's cut to the chase, what brings you to Tasco? They shut down all the pool halls over your way? Or did you kick everyone's ass in Paloma and you came lookin' for a real challenge?"

"I did come looking for something, but it wasn't for a game of eight-ball. I think we should probably go talk outside where it's a little less crowded."

"Geeze, fella. Take me out on a date first, will ya? You're not a cop now, are ya?" His tone of voice was a little more serious towards the end, so it was hard for me to tell if he was being facetious.

"Remember the time that biker broke a cue over your head and Mark knocked him out with an empty bottle of Scotch? You told him you owed him one. Well, even though he's not here anymore, I'm here to collect that debt for him."

"How could I forget? God rest his soul. Come on, let's step outside. I have a few minutes before it's my turn on the table."

As we went back out every eye followed us till we made it through the door. I would have loved to know what was going through everyone's mind. Most of the patrons were familiar faces and seeing me back after all this time looking for Lester would have sparked anyone's curiosity.

"I'm trying to find justice for what happened to my brother," I told him. "And I don't want to go into the specifics, but I need some of the best stuff you got, Lester. Probably enough to last a regular user a month."

"Yeah man, that won't be a problem. I got a lot of

good memories with your bro and so do most people inside. I don't mind doing this for him. When do you need it by?"

"I want it by tonight. But that's not all. I want double the amount in your special blend, the one you're famous for, if you know what I mean."

"Ahh. Now we're getting somewhere. I tell you what, let's go in and enjoy the tournament. Once it's over you can wait for me here and I'll make the run and drop it off."

"That sounds like a good idea. I just can't hang out afterwards. Mark's kids are with his neighbors tonight and everybody has to be up early tomorrow. They'll be waiting to get picked up. Plus, the drive back is a bitch."

"Don't sweat it, Eric. You'll be on your way soon after."

I didn't shoot any games that night, but being in the environment with old friends of mine and my brother brought back so many memories. It was fun catching up and hearing the friendly banter during the competition. Lester finished in third place and luckily for me he was in good spirits the whole time.

After nearly an hour and a half he went out to fetch me the goods and came back rather quickly. "Here you go, man." He handed me a shoebox through his car window. "Take good care of those kids. And you should come shoot some games with us every now and then. These guys miss ya hangin' out."

"That doesn't sound like a bad idea at all. I'll have to take you up on that." I reached for my wallet.

"No, no, don't worry about it. This one's on the house, for Mark. Do whatever you gotta do. I know how much he meant to you."

"You're a good guy, Lester. I'll see you around."

CHAPTER EIGHT

Even Loyalty Has a Price

I took the day off of work Wednesday to meet with Brenda at the park around noon and discuss what I wanted her to get out of Vicky. Hopefully everything continued to go as smoothly as it was going so far, but I always make sure to have a backup plan in case I hit a bump in the road.

As I drove up I almost didn't recognize her. She looked ten years older from the last time I had seen her and appeared to have lost close to thirty pounds. Her face was riddled with sores and I noticed a few bald spots on her head.

"Hey Brenda, looking good. How you been?" I asked her as she came over to my door.

"Just hangin' in there. Know what I mean? You? You brought it, right?" She glanced over to the passenger seat and into the back. "What's that box? Is that it?"

"Relax. Of course I brought it, I keep my word. And I want you to do the same. Come sit in the car and we'll have a talk." She went around the car and got in. I took the smaller bag from the box and handed it to her. "This is all yours right now. Go ahead, try it out."

She scooped some out of the bag with a tiny spoon and turned her nose into a vacuum cleaner. “What’s that other stuff in the box?” she asked. “It looks different.”

“That is your reward if you do exactly what I want. It’s a special blend that you’ve never tried before, and you’re not gonna want to miss it. I had to go very far to get my hands on that.”

“Why you doin’ all of this? What you tryin’ to do?”

“I’m not going to answer your questions. That wasn’t part of the deal.”

She leaned back against the headrest and closed her eyes as the drug began taking effect. “Damn, where did you get this stuff? You weren’t lying; this really is some good shit.” She reached for the baggy again.

“No, no, not till after we’re done talking. I don’t want you to start spazzing out on me. Listen to me very carefully. What has Vicky said about killing Mark? I want you to be real with me.”

“She was braggin’ about it to me one night when we were gettin’ high together. Told me he knocked on her door and questioned her about the gun she took from him. Said she gave him permission to search through her room and when he was in there she took her own gun out and shot him once at first. Mentioned how she was making him beg for his life and she shot him again. She was laughing the whole time she was telling me this.”

“Did she tell you why she decided to kill him?”

“I don’t remember everything, but I think she was talkin’ about how he didn’t wanna get back together and he already had a girlfriend.”

“What about the cuts on her head? How’d she get those?”

“Said she put some gloves on, took out his gun she

was hidin', and hit herself a few times with it then placed it in his hand. She wanted to make it look like he attacked her."

Her description of the events was the fuel I needed for the already burning fire within me. I knew I was doing the right thing and it would all be over soon. Patience was the key and I was running out of it, but I couldn't act on anything now and screw things up. I made a huge mistake once and it cost someone his life, and I wasn't going to do it again.

"All right, Brenda, pay real close attention to me. I'll write this down for you if I have to, just don't forget. When I leave here, I want you to call Vicky and tell her that you saw me and Detective Martinez having lunch together at the diner today. Tell her that you overheard me saying to Martinez that I had incriminating evidence locked up in my office safe at home that proves she killed my brother in cold blood."

"And then I get what's in that box?"

"Listen to me! I'm not done! You're not going to get anything if you mess this up. You heard us making a deal to meet up tomorrow morning at my place and that we couldn't do it sooner 'cause I was working on a project at home. Most importantly, tell her I said I'll be leaving at eight tonight to visit a friend in the hospital in Tasco. After you mention all of this, you have to make her say something to incriminate herself with Mark's murder. And don't get all paranoid and start acting suspicious. You got that?"

"We're good, I got it. I've done a lot more than that for a small fix."

"Oh, I'm not doubting that," I said.

"Can you give me a chance to try that other stuff real quick?" Her persistence was absolutely worth admiring.

Had she learned to use her talent for something positive there's no telling how far she could have gone.

"Get the fuck out of my car before I change my mind!" I snapped at her. "And let me know as soon as you do this and I'll bring you what I owe you. Don't screw it up, Brenda. If you forget anything I said you better call me *before* you talk to her. I don't want you to be mid conversation with her and say you'll have to call her back 'cause you forgot something."

It had been several hours and still no call from Brenda. *This idiot is probably having a party with every addict in a ten-mile radius*, I thought. Five o'clock was coming around and I was losing valuable time.

I needed to call Angelica and ask her if she could take care of Kate and Archer that evening once again. Maybe all the way into the next day if things went the way I had planned. The night was going to be a long one to say the least. I hated constantly having to bother her for help but there weren't many people I could turn to.

"Hey Eric, how are things going?"

"Going good, Angelica. Thanks for asking. I'm sorry for always hitting you up so unexpectedly, but things keep coming up all of a sudden."

"I already told you it's not a problem, whatever I can do for you guys I'm here."

"The kids will need a place to stay overnight. There are a few things I gotta take care of later today and I have no idea how long it will be until I can get 'em. I know you say it's OK; however, it still makes me feel like crap throwing them at you every chance I get."

"Don't worry about it," she insisted. "Seriously, they can stay here and I'll take them to school tomorrow if I have to."

"I'm not going to forget how much you're doing for me. Thank you."

"Hey Eric ... be careful."

Those last words caught me off guard and I assumed she somehow had a hunch something was going down that night. "I'll be fine, trust me. The kids will have everything they need for tomorrow. Thanks again."

A couple of minutes after I hung up my special agent finally decided to check in.

"Brenda, where the hell have you been? I've waited hours for your call."

"Sorry, Eric. Vicky wasn't pickin' up her phone until just 'bout fifteen minutes ago when I managed to get a hold of her. I called her every five minutes so don't think I had forg—"

"You called her every five minutes since we last saw each other? You don't think that was just a tad bit excessive and suspicious?" No matter how hard you try to keep it together there will always be people testing your patience, whether they know they're doing it or are simply utterly oblivious.

"She didn't make anything of it, I swear. I told her every single thing you wanted me to tell her and she got a lil panicky at first. Kept askin' me if you had mentioned what you had on her 'bout her killin' Mark."

"Well, did you get her to say anything incriminating that will show it wasn't self-defense?"

"She said how y'all ran into each other the other day and you really pissed her off and she wished she killed you too like she killed your brother."

"Brenda, that doesn't mean shit. That's still pretty useless."

"I'm gettin' to it, give me a second. She told me she can't wait to have you in front of her beggin' her not to kill you too. That she fooled all the cops and the DA already and doin' it one more time would be like a fun game for her."

Those words hit me like a cool breeze on a hot and humid summer afternoon. I felt genuinely proud of Brenda for accomplishing this small task.

"See, I knew I could count on you. You just gotta have some faith in yourself, woman, and something worth looking forward to."

"Can you drop off that stuff now? I'm at the park." Of course she was at the park. I had a feeling she had never left and wasn't going anywhere until I returned.

"Sure I will. You earned every bit of it. Don't go anywhere; I want you to be there when I show up."

"I ain't. Oh and Vicky also said that makin' it look like self-defense made her think she was on one of them criminal shows."

"Now you decide to remem—" I paused for a moment and took a deep breath. Talking with her made me feel like I was stuck in a comedy. "Forget it. I'll be there shortly."

I took my niece and nephew with me to the park so I could drop them off at Angelica's house after my meeting. Being home by eight was my target and I still needed to make a final long-distance drive to the neighboring county to pick up some acquaintances.

When I pulled up, Brenda went directly to the passenger side trying to get in, but I had locked the door before she could open it. "Ah! I'm just here to drop it off not have a chat. Come over here." I signaled for her to go around to my side.

She put her hands against the rear tinted windows to help her look inside and see who else was in the car.

"What are you doing?" I asked her.

"Hello," she said, waving at the kids through the glass with a huge grin on her face.

"Don't talk to 'em. You're going to scare them. Do you want this or not?" I handed her the box and turned the music up so my passengers couldn't hear anything I was going to say.

"Thanks for the help," I said. "It's just too bad the way things turned out. We could have all been a really big family and had some great times together."

"Yup, life's a bitch, ain't it?" She began to walk away then turned around to tell me one more thing. "Oh, Vicky always has a gun on her. She said she's not gonna go back to prison. So watch yourself."

I gave her a thumbs up.

"Uncle Eric, is she sick?" Kate asked.

"Yes, baby. But I just brought her some medicine. She won't feel a thing in a couple of hours."

I had dropped off the kids and was back on the road towards Madera County to pick up a couple of guys. Contacting Martinez was the last thing on my list so I figured I'd get that out of the way during the drive. It had been a little while since we last talked so I wanted to make the conversation the least awkward possible.

"Detective, how's your evening going? It's Eric."

"Hey Eric, how you been? How are things going?"

"They're going great actually. Listen, I was calling to ask you if anything new had come up with my brother's case. I had a dream about him last night and I figured I'd give you a call. Maybe he was trying to tell me something."

"I'm sorry, but I haven't run across anything new. I tried to get a hold of a few people who I thought were pretty close to Vicky and ask them some questions, and I wasn't able to reach them."

"I see. Do we still have a deal about reopening the case if we find new evidence like we discussed at the funeral?"

"Yeah, I gave you my word on that, Eric. You can call me anytime if you hear anything and I'll look into it. That's not going to change," he assured me.

"Thank you so much, it means a lot to me. By the way, I never got to show you my appreciation for the hard work you put into this case regardless of how it ended up. I play poker at my house Wednesday nights and have a few beers with friends, so if you're ever interested don't hesitate to swing by. In fact, I'm actually on my way to pick some of them up. I know it's last minute right now so maybe next week you can join us."

"I appreciate the invite, though I'm just not much of a poker guy. But maybe we can go have a drink sometime. I can take you up on that."

"Sounds good to me. You have yourself a good night, detective."

CHAPTER NINE

The Mark I Did Not Miss

The time was a quarter till eight when I eventually made it back home. I parked my car down the street and my two guests and I walked towards the house. It was an eerily quiet and cool evening without a single cloud in the sky, ideal weather to be sitting around a fire roasting marshmallows with the little ones. The night seemed too perfect for a handful of miscreants ready to disrupt the tranquility of such a pleasant neighborhood.

We walked inside and I made certain every door and window was locked and the home alarm system was disabled. My visitors received a clean set of clothes to change into and make themselves look more presentable. I grabbed a tray full of snacks and after turning off every light in the house we went into my office where I sat down behind my desk.

There was an old bottle of Scotch in one of the drawers and I pulled it out alongside a deck of cards from the times Mark and I used to play poker in the office. I remember one of those nights like it was just yesterday. Having taken almost all of his money, my brother decided it was a good idea to swing at me after several drinks. Even though that wasn't the only time I had kicked his ass playing cards, it was the only time since we were kids that he had gotten brave enough to actually fight me.

I kept looking at the clock and the passing of time felt twice as long as usual. Several thoughts popped into my head making me second-guess whether what I was doing was right, but reliving old memories I had with my family erased any doubt.

During several rounds of poker and in between shots with my company, I discussed almost everything with them that I had in mind for the next hour or so. It was only a matter of time before somebody else joined us to get the real party going. On the other hand, we were fifteen minutes from nine and I was starting to grow impatient.

As I shuffled the deck for the next game the neighbor's dog broke the silence with a sudden and profuse barking outside of the window. The blinds were closed, but I jumped up to cut the light and usher my guests into a small closet beside the door.

I went back to have a seat and make myself a little more comfortable. There were noises of breaking glass and things getting knocked over coming from the living room. My heart was racing so I flicked the top off of the bottle for a quick swig. The darkness wasn't helping the cause either and contributed to the unknown of what lay ahead.

Suddenly, I could hear footsteps slowly approaching the door and coming to a stop directly behind it. With a slight push it gradually swung open creaking its way along until it came to a halt. A figure stood silhouetted in the doorway against the now lit background and it was the discernible shape of a woman with long hair. She stood there for a brief moment and appeared to be almost hesitant to turn on the light.

Eventually, at the flip of the switch, she jumped

back letting out a shriek and holding her chest. "What the hell are you doing here!" she exclaimed. Fortunately for me she didn't have a weapon in her hands, meaning I had done an excellent job of making her think nobody was home.

"I live here. Oh, and I like meditating alone in the dark, it does wonders for my skin."

"Why isn't your car in the driveway?"

"What! It's not? My neighborhood crime watch was right; I need to start locking my vehicle. So what brings you to this side of my house?"

"Don't be stupid with me, Eric. What's in your safe? Someone told me you had somethin' in there that could put me in jail for what happened to your brother. That's what I'm here for." She reached behind her back and pulled out a pistol but held it down at her side. "I need you to stop tryin' to find somethin' on me. What's done is done. You can't bring your brother back."

I grabbed a shot glass and poured a drink, sliding it towards her on the desk. She shook her head so I shrugged it off and didn't let it go to waste. "You're right; alcohol's not healthy for you. Have a seat; let's have a little talk, something more productive than our conversation at the diner."

"I'm not here to talk. Just give me what I came here to get and I promise you I'll be on my way. This doesn't have to get ugly."

"Why did you do this to Mark? You knew damn well he had already left his old ways and you came in just to rip him away from us without a care. What was so hard about moving on, Vicky?"

"He did this to himself. All he had to do was take me back and I was willin' to change and become a good mother for the kids again."

"The kids don't even fuckin' remember you anymore. They're a lot happier now with somebody who actually provides the love and emotional support you could never give them. So don't talk about being a good mother. If you truly cared about them you would have understood that they had a more promising future with him, not with you. The only thing you've ever been good for is gettin' high with your lowlife friend, Brenda."

"Leave her out of this; she had nothin' to do with it."

"Oh, she had a lot to do with it," I reminded her. "Or did you forget it was her who introduced you to your shit and would bring you back at all hours of the night? You got lost in it and then you dragged my brother down with you."

"He was a grown man and could make his own choices. You didn't see him suffer like I did after your dad died. It took the pain away for a bit so he could forget about everything."

"And where the fuck is he now, Vicky! Huh! Where is he now! You cared so much about him to take his pain away back then, but you got rid of him to ease yours, right! Is that how it works!" I threw the shot glass over her head nearly striking her and she raised the gun at me. I had lost all fear now, I was in my zone.

"Open the safe and let me have what's in it and I'll leave. I have nothin' to lose so don't be stupid or you'll be the next one they bury. I can find my way out of this one too."

"You know, Archie didn't even want a birthday party anymore because his dad wasn't going to be there. I took him out to eat and get ice cream on his day and he spent most of the afternoon crying. Katie's had nightmares ever since and I've needed to get her a counselor to help her cope. Not that you care or anything. You have more important things in your life."

I noticed her eyes had begun to water and she tightened her grip on the gun. "Move over, I'll open it myself."

"What you're looking for is not in the safe. You probably have it on you right now. And from the looks of it, it's in your right pocket."

She looked down at her phone. "What the hell are you talkin' about?"

"That's the new one that just came out, right? You must have gotten a good deal on it. How's the camera? Carlos must have been really convincing when he called you."

"How do you know about this?" The tone of her voice was changing from her previous assertiveness to one of worry and confusion.

"Do you think it was a coincidence that shortly after your old phone went to shit in the restaurant a store calls a crackhead and says, 'Hey, take our newest phone home. We know you'll pay us later'?"

"What does that have to do with anything? Don't know what you're getting at."

"The phone was bugged before you picked it up, you idiot. The entire conversation you had with Brenda after she called you fifty times was recorded. The one where you told her that fooling the cops and the DA into believing it was self-defense made you feel like you were on some sort of a crime show. She was in on it herself." Her hand had developed a visible shake and I was waiting for the gun to go off any second.

"That's not true; she wouldn't do that to me. We go way back."

"And that's where you fucked up, trusting a junky like you. They'll betray you in a heartbeat for a fix. I don't have to convince you of that, you should know. It's all over now. The cops have the convo and your ass is going to rot in prison for the rest of your miserable life."

On that cue the closet doors swung open and the two men emerged from inside startling her. "Mrs. Acosta, we're with the police department, you're under arrest." Apparently they never realized she was indeed armed because their faces lit up at the sight of what she was holding.

In an instant she swung the gun around and let off four shots, dropping both of them. I reached under my desk and watched as her arm came back around in my direction. Time had seemingly slowed down and everything moved in slow motion in what would be the most important race of our lives.

I pulled my own steel and raised it just in time to fire one shot simultaneously with hers. My eyes closed and for a fraction of a second I saw my mom and dad alongside my brother, laughing with one another and having a good time. I was ready to go home and be welcomed into their arms, but I saw light once again and there was nobody in front of me any longer. Her shot had struck the headrest on my chair, slightly grazing my ear.

I could hear a faint wheezing emanating from someone on the floor so I got up and carefully made my way around the desk still clenching my gun. There was no sign of life in either of the men and then I saw Vicky. She no longer had the firearm in her hand and her eyes were staring at the ceiling while she struggled to breathe.

Kneeling down beside her I put my left hand behind her head and raised it just enough to keep her from drowning in her own blood. It brought back haunting memories of the hospital from the last time I saw my brother alive.

"Look at you," I whispered. "Look at the end result

of carrying so much vile hatred in your heart that you awakened the monster within me too. See, I've chosen to live my life peacefully and with love because only I know the destruction I'd be capable of had I gone your route of torment and evil. But sometimes fighting fire with fire is the only solution, and my fire burned with an unmatched fury compared to yours.

"There was no bug on your phone, Vicky. All I had to do was convince you that you were going back to prison for the rest of your life. I knew you wouldn't go back without a fight. These two guys aren't even cops. They're two homeless guys I picked up along the way who thought they were getting a place to stay tonight. God rest their souls, but in war there will always be collateral damage. I wasn't going to stop until I got what I wanted, and after what you told me in the restaurant, all I wanted since then was to watch you take your last breath.

"All the police will know is that you broke into my house and shot two of my unarmed friends playing cards and I had no choice but to put you down like the animal that you are. I lured you to your own death and the difference between this and what you did is that nobody will be coming after me like I came after you—because, frankly, nobody gives a shit about you. The only person who might have cared is most likely being zipped up in a body bag as we speak. Well, as *I* speak, 'cause you don't seem to have much to say now, do you? Poor Brenda, she really wanted that other stuff in the box. I was kind of starting to like her.

"By the way, the shot I offered you when you came in was on the house, a token of my hospitality. This second shot was courtesy of my brother Mark, and it wasn't an offer. So ... who was a step ahead of who, Vicky?"

On that note, she inhaled deeply and took her very

last breath, a closing statement to everything leading up to that moment.

I put the safety back on my gun.